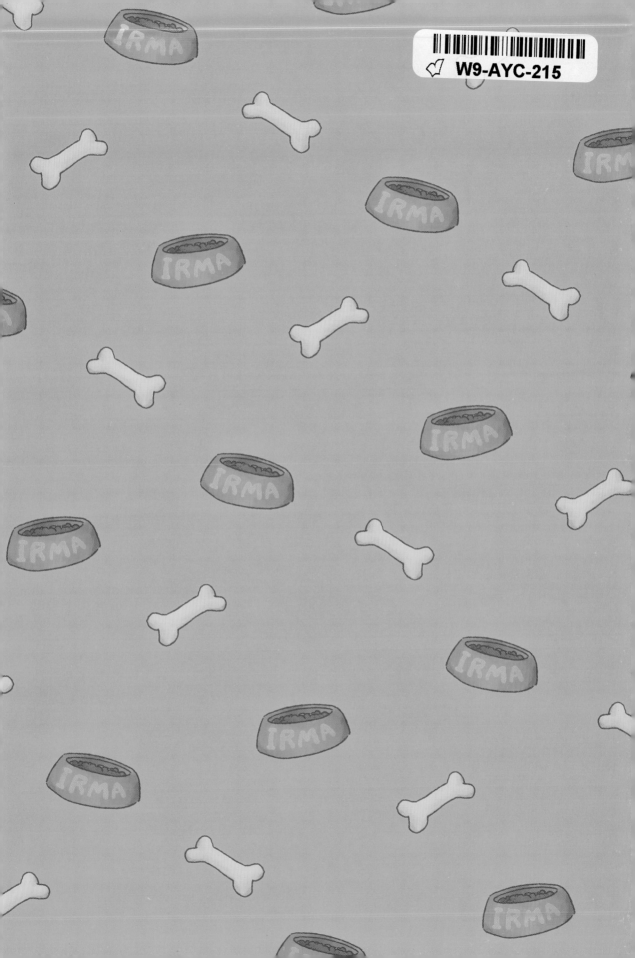

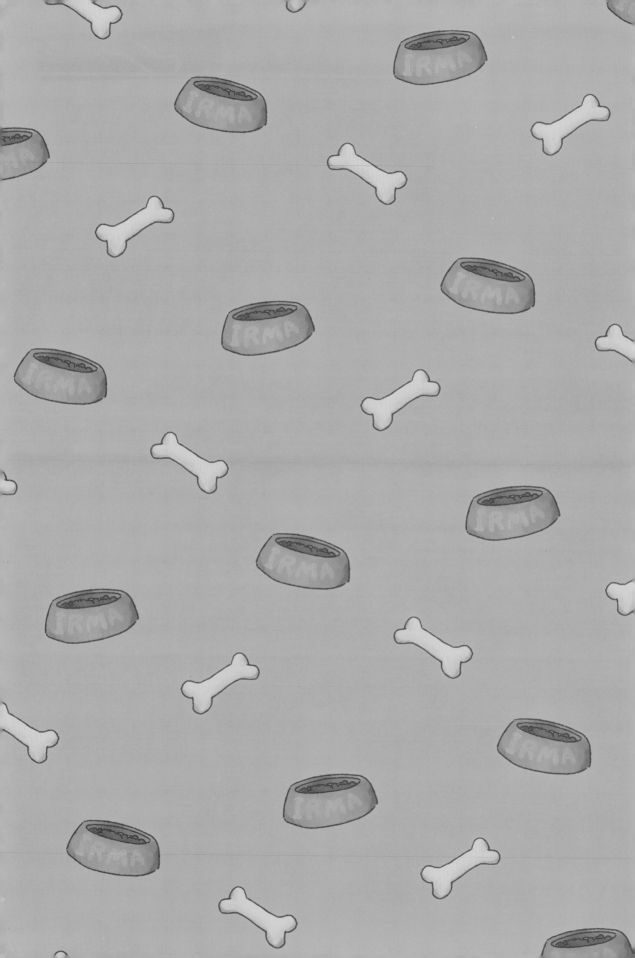

HEY, IRMA!
THIS IS HALLOWEEN

BY HARRIET ZIEFERT

PICTURES BY BARRY GOTT

Blue Apple Books

I'm Hank, and she's Irma.
Irma's not your ordinary dog.
She thinks she's a real person.

I'm hooked on computers, but I'm not a nerd. When I get home from school, I'm allowed "computer time." Right now, I'm sending an E-mail to my cousin, Lilly.

Dear Lilly,
I was in my room getting dressed for Halloween. I was rushing to go out trick-or-treating. And Irma really slowed me down...

I rushed around my room
finding stuff to wear.

First I pulled out
baggy blue pants...

and a plaid shirt.

Then I found
suspenders,

a purple
bow tie,

red sneakers,

and a big, old
cowboy hat.

I put everything neatly on my bed.
And who jumped on it? Irma!
I freaked and yelled at her.

Irma was insulted and hid under the bed.
But I knew she was watching my every move.

I put on my shirt and...

I pulled up my pants.

I tied my sneakers.

I fixed my suspenders.

I asked Irma what she thought of my outfit.

Irma, how do I look?

Irma did not answer or come out from under the bed, so I put on my bow tie. Again, I asked Irma for her opinion.

But Irma was still mad at me for yelling at her, and she did not even lift her tail.

I looked in the mirror.
I was not sure I liked the bow tie, so
I took it off and put on one of my dad's.
I asked Irma which one she preferred.

Irma did not answer. But...

she did come out from under the bed.
She pointed to the bow tie with her paw.

Irma, you prefer the bow tie.
Right? So I'll wear it!

Then Irma started to make unhappy noises. She whined. She cried. She yelped.

Irma ran to my dresser.
She barked. I asked myself,
   Now what does she want?

I opened the drawer.
Irma pulled out a plaid bow tie.

Irma pulled on the tie.
She held it and she
would not let it go.

Finally, I figured out that Irma
wanted to get dressed up too.

I grabbed my purple
trick-or-treat bag and
helped Irma with hers.

Out the door we went...
me first, then Irma.

For Jen, Jamie, & Sonny

Text copyright © 2003 by Harriet Ziefert

Illustrations copyright © 2003 by Barry Gott

CIP Data is available

Published in the United States 2003 by

Blue Apple Books

515 Valley Street, Maplewood, N.J. 07040

www.blueapplebooks.com

Distributed in the U.S. by Chronicle Books

First Edition

Printed in China

ISBN: 1-59354-022-1

1 3 5 7 9 10 8 6 4 2